student · secret agent · princess

PRINCESS NATASHA

student · secret agent · princess

#1 Cloning Around

Text by **Stephanie Peters**

Created by **Larry Schwarz**

Visit Princess Natasha every day at
www.princessnatasha.com.

Watch Princess Natasha on CARTOON NETWORK™
and anytime online on the KOL™ service at
KW: Princess Natasha.

LITTLE, BROWN & COMPANY
LB kids™
NEW YORK BOSTON LONDON
www.lb-kids.com

Text copyright © 2006 by Time Warner Book Group, Inc.

Illustrations by Animation Collective, Inc.

Little, Brown and Company

Time Warner Book Group
1271 Avenue of the Americas, New York, NY 10020
Visit our Web site at www.lb-kids.com

LB kids is an imprint of Little, Brown and Company Books for Young Readers, a
division of Time Warner Book Group. The logo design and name, LB kids, are
trademarks of Time Warner Book Group.

First Edition: May 2006

The characters and events portrayed in this book are fictitious. Any similarity to real
persons, living or dead, is coincidental and not intended by the author.

Based on the KOL™ cartoon created by Animation Collective

Library of Congress Cataloging-in-Publication Data

Peters, Stephanie True, 1965-
  Cloning around / text by Stephanie Peters.— 1st ed.
      p. cm.
  "Princess Natasha."
  "Based on the series created by Larry Schwarz."
  Summary: Natasha, secret agent and beloved princess of Zoravia, poses as an
exchange student in order to continue her battle against her evil uncle, Lubek, and
his clones.
  ISBN 0-316-15504-7 (pbk. : alk. paper)
  [1. Cloning—Fiction. 2. Spies—Fiction. 3. Princesses—Fiction.] I. Schwarz,
Laurence. II. Title.
PZ7.P441833Clo 2006
[Fic]—dc22

                                        2005014723

10 9 8 7 6 5 4 3 2 1

COM-MO

Printed in the United States of America

A Brief Zoravian History

Deep in the Carpathian Mountains lies the ancient kingdom of Zoravia. Usually, the people of this country live in peace and harmony. But there are times when darkness falls across this fair land—a darkness known as Lubek.

Fifteen years earlier, Lubek inherited control of Zoravia. But the people had long despised Lubek. They voted him off the throne and elected his brother, Carl, in his place.

Lubek fled to America and began scheming against his former homeland. For years, his exact whereabouts remained a mystery. Then Zoravian Intelligence discovered his secret identity. By day, Lubek works as a high school principal and science teacher in a small town in Illinois called . . . Zoravia.

Once known as Fountain Park, the town changed its name in honor of King Carl, Queen Lena, and their fourteen-year-old daughter, Princess Natasha. Natasha had never met her evil uncle, but she had spent her life preparing to defeat him.

And now, she'll have her chance. Trained as a secret agent, Natasha has come to Illinois, where she poses as an exchange student at Fountain Park High. No one—not her host family, her friend Maya, or her fellow students—can ever know her true identity. If Lubek ever found out who she was, it would be the end of Natasha—and her beloved Zoravia.

Chapter One

Flower Power

Natasha—princess of Zoravia, secret agent, and high school exchange student—wasn't afraid of a challenge. After all, she had battled evil countless times. But nothing so far had prepared her for what she now faced.

"We have to make *three hundred* tissue paper flowers by *tomorrow?*"

Natasha stared in dismay at the stacks of flimsy paper on the kitchen table. The flowers were for the "April Showers Bring Zoravian

Flowers" exhibit, an annual celebration to welcome the coming of spring to their town and the country of Zoravia. "How can we possibly make that many flowers in one night?"

"*We?*" Greg O'Brien, the handsome teenage son of Natasha's American host parents, leaned against the door frame. "Who said anything about *we?*" He flashed a brilliant white smile at his girlfriend, Kelly. "You ready?"

Kelly smoothed a wrinkle from her miniskirt, fluffed her blond hair, and nodded.

Natasha jumped up. "Hey! Where are you guys going?"

"Movie," Greg drawled.

"It's a love story." Kelly tucked her arm around Greg's waist and smirked.

Natasha pointed a finger at Kelly. "You can't leave! Making these stupid flowers was *your* idea."

Kelly shot her an exasperated look. "Then I've obviously *done* my part. I mean, hello? Coming up with that idea was really . . . you know . . . " She  searched the ceiling for the right word. "Really *hard*," she finally finished.

Natasha turned to Greg. "Didn't you tell your parents you'd keep an eye on KC tonight?" She glanced over to where the O'Brien's younger son was playing video games.

Greg shrugged. "I told my parents that 'one
of us'"—he made air
quotes with his fin-
gers—"would keep
an eye on him. And
you *are* 'one of us'—
air quotes again—
"aren't you?"

"Yes, but—"

"When you think about it," Kelly interrupted,
"it makes perfect sense for you
to watch KC."

Natasha crossed her arms.
"How do you figure?" *This
should be good,* she thought.

"Because you're going to
be here making flowers anyway!" Kelly gave Greg a triumphant
look. He flashed her a double thumbs-up.

Natasha gave up. "Fine, leave," she said.

"I'll—"

SLAM! Kelly and Greg were out the door, without a backward glance.

Natasha sighed, picked up a tissue, and pleated it into a flower. *One down, two hundred and ninety-nine lame decorations to go.*

"What's this?"

KC had come into the kitchen. He picked up the flower, put it to his nose, and inhaled deeply. Suddenly, his face twitched.

"Aaaahhhh . . . AAAA . . . *AAAHHHH . . .*"

Natasha ducked just as KC exploded with a powerful sneeze.

" . . . CHOOOO!"

He wiped his nose with the back of his hand and then examined the flower with great interest. "It caught my boogers," he announced.

"Gross. Throw it away," Natasha said.

"Throw it away?" KC echoed in alarm. "This is prime nose debris! I'm adding it to my collection." He scraped a fingernail through the mess.

Natasha cringed. Back home in Zoravia, she'd be watching a movie with her friends, reading a good book, or maybe even dancing at a ball given in her honor. Here, she was watching a nine-year-old collect snot.

Aah, the glamorous life of a secret agent.

Just then, she heard a muffled voice coming from her bedroom.

KC looked up. "Who's that?" he asked.

"Nobody!" Natasha backed out of the room. "I'll go check it out. You keep working on your—uh—project." She closed the door and took the stairs two at a time.

She knew exactly what the sound was. Someone was trying to contact her on her Booferberry telecommunicator. When that happened, it meant one thing: Lubek, the number one enemy of her beloved Zoravia, was up to no good.

Chapter Two

Trouble Times Two . . . or Three . . . or Four?

Natasha shut the door to her room and pulled out her Booferberry.

"You've got an alert!" it intoned.

She pushed a button. The image of her father materialized on the small screen.

"Natasha, my dear!" King Carl said. "Is all well with you?"

Natasha nodded. "Yes, Daddy, I'm fine. What's my new assignment?"

The king looked grim. "Take a look at this!"

A small rectangular device with a single large button appeared on the screen next to him.

"It looks like a one-channel television remote," Natasha said.

"Not quite," King Carl said. "This is a Zy-Clone. It makes clones."

"It *what*?"

"Makes clones," her father repeated. "When you point it at an object and push the button, it creates a double of that object."

"Impossible!"

"Possible!" the king corrected. "Zoravian scientists developed the technology years ago, when our yak population was dying out. You know how important yaks are to Zoravia. They had to be saved, no matter what. But the cloning project was soon abandoned."

Natasha nodded. "They realized that it was wrong to tamper with the natural order of things," she guessed.

"No. Like you, people thought the Zy-Clone was a remote. Zoravia was nearly buried under a mountain of cloned TVs." Her father shuddered

at the memory. "Also, yak clones turned out to be, well, not too smart. They had to be told what to do. Unfortunately, the real yaks refused to help. So the shepherds had to demonstrate everything—how to eat, when to sleep, how to, er, make dung."

"I get the picture," Natasha said dryly. "So what happened?"

"Luckily, the clones didn't last long. They faded away after about a month."

"Faded away?"

"Went from solids to gases. Methane gas, actually."

"And what about the cloning technology?"

"The scientists were supposed to destroy everything related to the project. It seems they didn't." His voice fell to a whisper. "Lubek has made a Zy-Clone. He's building an army of Lubek clones!"

Natasha gasped.

"Contact Oleg immediately, Natasha. He knows where Lubek's lab is."

"I'm on it! Natasha out!" Natasha hung up and then quickly dialed Oleg.

Oleg Boynski was her spy partner. When he appeared on her screen, he straightened his lab coat and peered at her anxiously through  round, thick-rimmed glasses. (Oleg was a technology whiz and a top secret agent, but he had a thing or two to learn about fashion.) Natasha quickly outlined the situation.

"Dad said you know where Lubek's lab is."

Oleg nodded. "An abandoned mirror factory on the far side of town."

Natasha knelt in front of the secret drawer where her spy suit was hidden. "Then what are we waiting for? Let's—"

Suddenly she froze, cocked her head to one side, and sniffed. A moment later, earsplitting shrieks from a smoke alarm filled the air.

Uh-oh. "Gotta go, Oleg. I'll call back when I can!"

She shut off the Booferberry and then rushed downstairs. Black smoke curled from beneath the kitchen door.

"KC!" She pounded on the kitchen door. "KC, are you in there?"

The door swung open. "'S up?" KC asked calmly.

Natasha pushed him aside. "What happened?"

KC jerked a thumb at a charred lump inside the microwave. "I nuked some popcorn." He took out the bag and shook it. Sooty flakes fluttered to the ground. "I like it well-done."

Natasha made a face. "Ugh, the whole kitchen reeks of burned popcorn!"

KC inhaled deeply. "Yeah," he said with a happy sigh. "They should bottle that smell." He tossed a handful of blackened bits into his mouth and then opened the refrigerator.

Natasha rolled her eyes. She started tugging at the nearest window to let in some fresh air.

Thud.

Natasha looked over her shoulder. A big bottle of orange soda had fallen from the refrigerator. KC spun it a few times, picked it up, and carried it to the table.

Natasha shook her head and yanked at the window again. Then she paused.

He wouldn't—

FFFFFFssssssttt—WHOOOSH!

Orange liquid sprayed her arms, hair, and clothes.

He would. She turned to look at KC.

Sticky soda dripped from his face—and from the table, the walls, and the ceiling. Puddles were forming on the floor. He looked delighted.

Natasha groaned. "KC, when you drop a full bottle of soda, you have to open it slowly so it doesn't explode!"

"Or," KC responded, "you can open it fast so it does!"

Natasha pulled a long strip of paper towels from a roll, wet it, and started wiping her face and arms clean. *Can this night possibly get any worse?* she wondered.

Upstairs, the Booferberry started jangling again.

Enter the Clones

"Oleg, you're on your own with this one. If I leave KC alone, he'll destroy the entire house." She heard a loud crash from the kitchen and shook her head.

Oleg squared his shoulders and stood tall—or as tall as a man of his small stature could stand. "Don't worry, Princess. I shall render Lubek defenseless and save Zoravia. Ho! Ha, ha!" He judo-chopped the air and whirled in a spin kick. Pens flew from his lab coat pocket protector.

Natasha hid a smile. "Just to be safe, I'm going to keep an eye on you on the Lubek Locator."

The Locator was a handy computer that had helped her find Lubek many times. It scanned an area, identified anything that looked like Lubek and then tracked his movements on the screen. It was usually accurate—although one time it had mistakenly identified a circus sideshow performer known as the Bald Lady as Lubek.

Natasha typed the address of the mirror factory into the Locator. A moment later, a map of the factory's street came

on the screen. There was no sign of Lubek. Natasha zoomed in on the factory itself. A blueprint of the building's interior popped up. Again, no Lubek.

"Hmm, he's not there," she said. "Oleg, e-mail me that image of the Zy-Clone. I'm going to program the Locator to look for it in the factory."

Oleg sent the file and she typed in the necessary commands. A moment later, a small yellow blip appeared on the screen.

Natasha grinned. "Bingo! The Zy-Clone is there. You should be able to get in, grab it, and get out without a problem. Still . . . "

She typed a few more commands. "I've programmed you into the Locator, too, Oleg. You'll appear as a green blip."

Oleg frowned.

"What's wrong?"

"I want to be blue."

Natasha sighed but pressed a few more buttons. "Okay, you're blue. Satisfied?"

Oleg smiled happily. "I shall report back once I have the Zy-Clone. Oleg out."

His image shrank to a pinpoint and then vanished. Natasha closed her Booferberry and glanced at her watch.

It'll take him a while to get to Lubek's lab, she thought. *Enough time for me to clean the kitchen and KC.*

She hurried downstairs. For fifteen minutes, she wiped soda from the counters and walls and mopped it from the floor. She salvaged as much of the tissue as she could and carried it to her room. Then she found KC and hauled him off to the bathroom.

"But I *like* being sticky!" he complained as she turned on the shower. He showed her a huge ball of dust and hair attached to his pants.

"See this? Think of the other cool stuff that could stick to me!"

"Ugh!" She shoved him under the water.

"Hey, I've still got my clothes on!" he yelled. Then—"Pass me the laundry soap! I'm gonna agitate!"

"Trust me, you're already agitating," Natasha said under her breath. She left him making sounds like the chugging of a washing machine.

In her room, she checked the Locator. Two blips, a blue one and a yellow one, appeared on the screen. Oleg had reached the factory.

Suddenly, the screen changed. Instead of one blue blip, dozens appeared! Then, as quickly as they had materialized, all but one vanished.

Natasha sat back in confusion. Was her

Locator on the blink?

Then she snapped her fingers. "Of course! Lubek's secret lair is in a mirror factory. I'll bet there are mirrors everywhere. The Locator must have identified Oleg's reflections as real Olegs."

The Locator flashed multiple blue blips two more times. Natasha kept her eye on the one that remained when the others disappeared. That blip moved slowly and steadily toward the cloning device until, at last, it was right next to it. A moment later, the two blips started moving together.

Yes! Oleg has the Zy-Clone! She flopped back on her bed in relief.

The Locator gave a harsh beep. Natasha sat up. A bright orange blip had appeared. *Lubek!*

Sock It to Me

The blue and yellow blips stopped moving. Natasha guessed Oleg had spotted Lubek. She wondered if Lubek had seen Oleg.

A moment later, many more orange blips popped onto the screen. *Reflections*, she thought.

Then she frowned. Something wasn't right. Unlike Oleg's blue blips, which had appeared and disappeared quickly, the orange blips stayed steady.

Oh, man, those aren't Lubek reflections! she realized in horror. *They're Lubek clones!*

She tore open the drawer that hid her spy suit. She was about to pull it out when *splot!*—a wet sock soared across the room and wrapped itself around her head.

"Gotcha!" KC, still in his sopping wet clothes, ran from the room, hooting with laughter.

Natasha hurled the sock to the floor. "One of these days, KC, I'm going to—"

Crash!

"Ow!" KC bellowed.

"*Now* what?" Natasha rushed to the hallway. KC was sprawled at the bottom of the stairs.

Visions of a trip to the hospital danced in her

head. "Did you break anything?" she called.

"Just a lamp." He stood up. "Know what? You can slide *really* fast down the banister when your clothes are wet, but"—He tugged at the seat of his pants—"you get the mother of all wedgies. Yow!" He squished his way up the stairs to his room.

She was about to follow him when she heard a loud thump coming from her room! She instantly dropped to a crouch. Heart pounding, Natasha edged along the wall to her door and listened.

No doubt about it. Someone was moving around in her room.

She laid a hand on her doorknob; took several quick, deep breaths; then—

"*Yee-haaaaah!*"

With a loud yell, she shoved open the door, somersaulted inside, and sprang up to a fighting stance. Fists at the ready, she searched for the intruder. She found him crumpled under the window. It was Oleg.

She hurried to his side. "What happened?"

Oleg pulled KC's soggy sock from beneath him.

27

"I slipped on this when I climbed in." He wrinkled his nose. "You should take better care of your clothes, Natasha."

She took the sock and threw it into a corner. "I meant, what happened at the factory?"

He handed her a small, rectangular object. "I succeeded."

"Good work! But what about the Lubek clones?"

Oleg shuddered. "They were everywhere! Hundreds of them!"

Natasha raised an eyebrow. "Really? The Locator didn't show quite that many."

Oleg cleared his throat. "Well, perhaps not hundreds. Maybe ten. Anyway, I escaped their terrible clutches, as you can see."

"How?"

"I recently turbocharged my scooter," he said proudly.

"Nice! Did Lubek or his clones follow you?"

"I don't think so."

"Then they might still be at the factory."

She checked the Lubek Locator. There were no blips of any color on the screen. She zoomed out to see if any appeared outside the factory. Nothing.

"Rats. We lost him, er, them." She turned her attention to the Zy-Clone. "What does this number mean?"

"What number?"

She pointed to a small red 2 near one end.

"Hmmm. Let me examine it more closely," he said.

Natasha gave him the Zy-Clone.

ZAP!

A bright beam of green light flashed across the room and struck KC's sock.

"Oops!" Oleg looked sheepish. "I think I pushed the button."

They stared at the sock. Or rather, socks. Where there had been only one a moment before, there were now two.

Chapter Five

Two Places, One Natasha

Natasha picked up the cloned sock. "Amazing!" she said.

"Indeed!" Oleg glanced at the cloning device. "Aaaah!" he cried. "The number has changed from 2 to 1!"

Natasha looked from the sock to the Zy-Clone and back again. "Hmmm. I'll bet that number indicates how many more clones this thing can make. That means there's just enough juice left for one more." She smiled at

Oleg. "You know, if not for your good work, we'd have to defeat two *more* Lubeks."

Oleg blushed.

Natasha started pacing. "Okay, it's time to figure out what we're going to do."

Just then, they heard KC make his way down the stairs, singing at the top of his lungs. The singing stopped abruptly and was replaced by noise from the television.

Oleg shifted uneasily. "Excuse me, Natasha," he said, "but how can you help me defeat Lubek and his clones when you must stay with KC? You can't be in two places at the same time."

Natasha looked at the Zy-Clone in her hand. "Can't I?"

Oleg's jaw dropped. "You mean, make a clone—of *yourself*?"

"One of me stays here, the other goes with you."

"I don't like it, Natasha!"

"You have a better idea?"

He stared at her and then shook his head.

"Okay, then." She slowly turned the Zy-Clone toward herself.

"Wait!" Oleg cried. He sat down at her desk and booted up her computer.

She stood behind him. "What are you doing?"

"I'm hacking into Zoravia's top secret science files. It's probably where Lubek got the information to build the Zy-Clone in the first place." He typed some more. "Your father said the yak clones eventually faded away, right? Well, maybe I can figure out a way to program the Zy-Clone to speed up the fade-out."

"Great idea, Oleg!"

Moments later, the screen was filled with mathematical equations. "Interesting. It runs on batteries," Oleg murmured. He scanned the

$45a + 25ab/4z^2 = 85a-25x^3b7\%25<5z^2x^3b$
$36.751 * 32ab^2 + 475.32\ xy^3\ 98/72.4\ 4>3$
$425.76 = 456a^3y^2\ 72/42\ a^2b^2 + 142xy$
$45a + 25ab/4z^2 = 85a-25x^3b7\%25<5z^2x^3b$
$36.751 * 32ab^2 + 475.32\ xy^3\ 98/72.4\ 4>3$
$425.76 = 456a^3y^2\ 72/342\ a^2b^2 + 142xy$
$45a + 25ab/4z^2 = 85a-25x^3b7\%25<5z^2x^3b$
$36.751 * 32ab^2 + 475.32\ xy^3\ 98/72.4\ 4>3$
$425.76 = 456a^3y^2\ 72/42\ a^2b^2 + 142xy$
$36.751 * 32ab^2$

computations some more, grunted once and then pushed a button. The screen went blank.

"Well?" Natasha asked.

"I can reprogram the Zy-Clone," Oleg announced confidently. "Also, I have eradicated the files so that they can never be accessed again."

"Then it's showtime." Without another word, Natasha turned the device on herself and pushed the button.

Green light filled the room again. Then—

"It's like looking in a mirror!"

Natasha stared at her double. The clone stood slack-jawed, arms hanging limply at her sides. Her eyes were dull.

"A mirror that makes me look like I have a brain the size of a walnut," Natasha amended. "It's a little weird."

"You get changed," Oleg said. "I shall begin the reprogramming." He pulled out a screwdriver and started to dismantle the device.

Natasha ducked into her closet, changed into her spy suit, and bounded out with a determined look on her face.

"Let's go!" she cried.

Oleg pointed the screwdriver at the other Natasha. "She needs her instructions first."

"Oh yeah." Natasha stood in front of the

clone. "Your instructions are to watch KC. Understand? You—"

She jabbed a finger into the clone's shoulder.

"watch—"

She pointed two fingers at her eyeballs.

"KC."

She pantomimed a person sticking a finger up his nose.

The clone yawned, scratched her backside, and lumbered into the hallway.

Natasha rolled her eyes. "A fine specimen, that one."

From the bed the Lubek Locator beeped, making them both jump. Orange Lubek blips filled the screen.

"They're ba-a-ack!" Oleg said.

Chapter Six

Send in the Clones

Natasha and Oleg vaulted out the window, swung from a large tree branch to the ground, and hurried to Oleg's scooter.

"I'll drive," Natasha said. "You keep working on the Zy-Clone."

Within minutes, they were outside the mirror factory. Natasha stowed the scooter in an alley and then joined Oleg, who was hiding in some shrubs.

"How's it coming?" she whispered. The device was still in pieces.

"A little longer," Oleg muttered. He fit one piece into another, tinkered with some wires and then pulled two new C-sized batteries from his pocket. He inserted them into the Zy-Clone and snapped the cover into place. "There! This now has enough power to take care of one clone."

"Just one?"

Oleg patted a pocket on his lab coat. "Don't worry. I always carry extra batteries, in case of emergencies."

Natasha couldn't imagine what kind of emergency might require a stash of C batteries, but she chose not to ask. "Okay, let's see what we're up against." She tiptoed to an open window, pressed her back against the wall, and slid upward until she could see inside.

The factory was one large room with a high ceiling. It was dimly lit by a single overhead bulb. Mirrors of various shapes and sizes lined the large room's walls and stood propped against tables. Shambling among the mirrors were the Lubek clones.

"I count fifteen of them," she whispered to Oleg. "No wait, twenty-two. No, hold it, there are only thirteen!" She growled in frustration. "It's those mirrors again! I don't know if I'm seeing reflections or clones!"

Oleg pointed to the pair of high-tech, super-powered glasses attached to her utility belt. "Put those on and switch them to heat mode. They should detect the real clones' body heat."

Natasha did as he suggested and peeked again. "It's working. There are actually only seven clones."

"Can you see the real Lubek?"

Natasha scanned the room. "I don't think so. The ones I see are all acting like the clone I left at home. You know, stupid and robotic."

Just then a voice boomed out. "Clones," it said, "this is your master speaking!"

Natasha and Oleg exchanged glances. "Lubek! He's in there," Oleg said.

Natasha peeked again. "Hold it, I see him. He was standing in the shadows. Listen!"

"You must locate and retrieve the missing device," Lubek told his clones. "Half of you will search the west side of town. The other half will search the east. Any questions?"

The Lubek clones shifted and looked at one another. One of them raised a hand.

"Speak!" Lubek bellowed.

"There are seven of us," the clone said. Lubek frowned."Yes, so?"

"Seven can't be split in half."

"Gaaah!" Lubek slapped his forehead with his hand. "Stupid clones." He jabbed a finger at four of the Lubeks. "Okay, you, you, you, and you go west. The other three go east. Understand?"

Another clone raised a hand. "What?!"

The clone pointed at a mirror hanging close by. "What about him?"

Lubek threw his arms up in disgust. "We've been over this! That is just your reflection!" He marched to the mirror and flipped it over.

"See? He's gone."

The clone lifted a corner of the mirror and peered into it. "No, he's still there."

Lubek tore at his hair. "Just go find the device and bring it to me!"

"But what about him?" the clone insisted.

"He's going to stay here! Now go!"

The clones started to shuffle toward the door.

"Oleg," Natasha whispered urgently, "we have to get them now, before they split up!"

Oleg laid the thumb of one hand on the Zy-Clone's button and palmed two spare batteries in his other hand. "I'm ready."

"Then let's do it!"

Chapter Seven

Mirror, Mirror, on the Wall

"Keee-aaii!"

Natasha and Oleg burst through the window. Natasha landed next to a clone and dealt him a swift side kick to the stomach.

"Oof!" The clone stumbled backward and fell against a mirror. The mirror crashed to the floor and shattered into a thousand pieces.

Oleg pointed the Zy-Clone at him. ZAP! Blue light filled the room.

Natasha looked to where the clone had fallen.

The spot was empty. "It worked!" she called.

Oleg didn't answer. He was too busy changing batteries.

Natasha detected a movement on her right. She spun and delivered a one-two punch to another clone's rib cage.

"Oof, oof!" the second clone grunted.

ZAP! The second clone vanished in a blaze of blue light.

"Five to go!" Natasha shouted. She bounced on her toes, expecting the clones to attack.

But the five remaining Lubeks

simply stood still.

They're waiting for instructions! Natasha thought. *Maybe I can tell them what to do!*

But just as that thought crossed her mind, Lubek's voice boomed out again.

"Clones, I command you to grab the intruders!"

Instantly, the five Lubeks lurched toward her with their arms outstretched.

It's like something from a bad zombie movie! Natasha thought as they closed in.

Luckily, her spy suit had features to help her out of such predicaments. With a touch of her Zero Gravity Elbow Pad, she rocketed up to the ceiling, somersaulted over the clones' heads, and landed feetfirst behind them.

The five clones blinked in bewilderment.

"Gaarrgh!" Lubek shouted. "Dimwits! Forget her! Find the one who is erasing you and stop him! He's hiding behind that big mirror in the corner!"

Natasha sprang in front of the mirror. "I got you covered, partner," she called to Oleg.

ZAP!

"Likewise," Oleg responded as another Lubek disappeared. Natasha heard two clunks and a click and knew he had changed batteries again.

"Four against one," she murmured as the clones turned toward her. "Those are odds I can handle. Although . . . "

She glanced at a stack of mirrors laying next to her. She remembered how one of the clones had been confused by his reflection. *Maybe I can trick them into thinking there are more of me! While they attack my reflection, I can attack them!*

She quickly positioned two mirrors on either side of her. With the one behind her, they formed a three-way looking glass with a Natasha reflection in each one.

"Bring it on," she muttered. "My sisters and I are ready."

Her plan seemed to work. The four clones halted, obviously confused by the sudden appearance of more opponents.

"What are you waiting for?" Lubek shouted. "Attack!"

The clone to Natasha's right pulled back his fist then slammed it into her reflection's face.

Ouch, Natasha thought as the mirror splintered.

ZAP! The clone disappeared.

"Three against three! Still a fair fight!" Natasha cried.

The clone directly in front of her charged. She stood her ground until the last minute, then nimbly stepped aside.

SMASH!

ZAP!

"Two to go!" Natasha yelled.

"Make that three!"

From out of nowhere, a new Lubek appeared. It only took Natasha a second to realize that this one wasn't a clone.

With an evil laugh, Lubek pulled what looked like a very dangerous, very *deadly* laser gun from his belt and pointed it directly at

Natasha's heart.

"Now *you* shall be erased!" And he pulled the trigger.

Chapter Eight

Laser Tag

Natasha dropped to the floor and rolled sideways just as the laser fired. She was on her feet and running when the beam struck the mirror. To her amazement, the laser bolt didn't shatter the mirror. Instead it reflected off at an angle, struck another mirror on the other side of the room, bounced off again, and finally hit a wall where it burned a hole through to the outside.

Lubek looked from the gun to the mirror in

surprise. "Interesting," he said.

"Interesting," repeated the two remaining clones.

ZAP! One remaining clone.

"Gah!" Lubek yelled. He shoved the last clone toward Oleg's hiding place. "You, get him! I will go after the other! And try not to get de-cloned, will you?"

Clunk. Clunk. Click. ZAP! Now the blue light came from a different corner.

"And then there were none," Natasha murmured. Oleg peeked out and gave her a thumbs-up.

Lubek whirled around and around. When he realized he was alone, he gave a shriek of frustration. Then he spotted Oleg. "You will pay for this!" he cried, raising the laser once more.

"Look out!" Natasha cried.

Oleg threw himself behind a squat mirror just in time. The laser beam ricocheted off the shiny surface and shot through a wall instead of through Oleg.

Now Lubek spun and aimed at Natasha. She dodged the bolt thanks to the Zero Gravity

Elbow Pad. The laser ripped a hole in the ceiling. A second beam narrowly missed her as she flipped through the air. She landed and  dashed behind the nearest mirror. It was a full-length, freestanding, oval-shaped beauty, rimmed with mahogany wood and set in a frame that allowed it to tilt up and down.

Kelly would love this thing, Natasha thought. She gripped its sides. When Lubek fired at her, she tilted it. The beam was deflected up through the hole in the ceiling. *Gotta admit I'm kind of loving it right now myself!*

Lubek shot the laser three more times. Twice Natasha sent the beam through the hole in the ceiling. The third time, she accidentally deflected it at the one light in the place. The bulb shattered and the room was plunged into near darkness.

Lubek stopped firing.

The abrupt silence made Natasha more uneasy than the laser blasts had. *What's he up to?* she wondered. She started to peek around the mirror then stopped. *That's just what he wants me to do, I'll bet.*

The seconds ticked by. She strained her ears, knowing even the smallest sound would give Lubek away.

But the sound she heard next wasn't small. It was *deafening.*

CRASH! CRASH! CRASH!

He's breaking the mirrors! Natasha realized. *And when he's broken them all, Oleg and I will be helpless against his weapon! I've got to stop him.*

Holding her breath, she slowly inched her way from behind the mirror and crouched against the wall. Even in the dim light, she spotted Lubek right away. He was carrying a broom  stick and heading toward another mirror.

Something stirred across the room. A short figure in a white lab coat moved across the floor. Oleg was sneaking toward Lubek.

He might have made it, too, if he hadn't stepped on a piece of broken mirror.

CRUNCH! The sound of glass underfoot broke the silence. Lubek whirled, saw Oleg, and let out a wicked laugh.

Chapter Nine

A "Thock" in the Dark

"Well, well, well . . . " Lubek pointed the laser at Oleg's head. He reached forward and pulled the Zy-Clone from Oleg's hand. "Why, I do believe this belongs to me!"

"It does *not* belong to you!" Oleg bristled. "You stole it from the people of Zoravia!"

Lubek narrowed his eyes. "They stole something from me, too. My throne!"

"You didn't deserve the throne," Oleg replied. "And you know why, don't you!"

"Perhaps," Lubek said. "So why don't you tell me?" Oleg goaded.

Natasha realized that Oleg was trying to distract Lubek so she could make her move! *Good work,* she thought. *Now if I can just find something that could help us.*

Her gaze landed on a small cylindrical object near her feet. It was a dead battery. She slowly lowered her hand and picked it up. Using the shadows as cover, she ducked behind a mirror, slipped a slingshot from her utlility belt, and fit the battery in it.

She would have one chance. Lubek was facing her. If she launched the battery just right, she could hit him between the eyes. She might even knock him out.

Here goes nothing! She stood up, pulled

back on the slingshot band, and let go. The battery soared across the room, making a bee-line straight for Lubek's shiny, bald cranium.

THOCK!

"Ow!"

"Oops!"

At the last minute, the battery had dipped downward and struck Oleg in the back of the head. He staggered forward into Lubek. Lubek

toppled back-ward and hit the floor with a loud thud. The laser and the Zy-Clone skit-tered across the floor.

Natasha dashed across the room and

scooped up the gun and the Zy-Clone before Lubek could retrieve them. She knelt down

next to Oleg and rolled him gently to his back.

"Oleg! Oleg! Are you okay?"

He blinked a few times. "I'm seeing stars."

"Don't move. I'll take care of you once I've taken care of—Oh no!"

She looked up just in time to see Lubek climb out a window and vanish into the night.

"You got away this time," she growled. "But

just you wait. We'll get you yet."

She turned back to Oleg.

"Do you think you can sit up?"

"I—I don't know." He stared skyward. "I am still seeing stars. Different stars, but stars."

Natasaha looked up. Directly above Oleg was the hole in the ceiling. "Um, Oleg, I think those are *real* stars you're seeing."

"Oh." He sat up and rubbed the back of his head. "That would explain why they formed the Orion constellation."

"Are you well enough to move?" she asked.

He tried to stand but sank back down to the floor. "I think maybe I'd better stay here a while longer." He smiled. "But you go. You don't want any of the O'Briens to return and find your clone, do you?"

Natasha had forgotten all about her clone. A quick glance at her watch told her that Oleg was right; if she didn't hurry, someone else would be home before she was!

She left Oleg the laser gun but took the Zy-Clone with her.

"Just point and zap," Oleg instructed her as he gave her two C batteries.

Natasha sped home on the scooter as fast

as she could. Once there, she climbed the tree to her window, crawled into her room, and changed into her regular clothes. Then she went in search of her double.

Chapter Ten

Clones to the Rescue!

Natasha had expected to hear the sounds of the television, the stereo, video games, or even all three from the rooms downstairs. But the house was silent. Ominously so.

She cracked open her door and listened carefully. At last, she heard a noise. It was coming from the bathroom.

"I gotta go!" she heard KC say.

"I—watch—KC."

"You're not gonna watch me *pee!*"

Natasha peeked down the hallway. The clone stood in front of the bathroom, one hand pushing the door open wide.

"I—watch—KC."

"Listen," KC whimpered, "I've been holding it all night! Can't you just leave me alone for one second?!"

Stifling a laugh, Natasha waved her arm until she caught the clone's attention. She signaled for the clone to come to her room. The clone lurched away from the bathroom to Natasha's room.

"Finally!" KC yelled as he slammed the bathroom door shut.

In her room, Natasha picked up the Zy-Clone and aimed it at her double. One flash of blue later, she was alone.

But not for long. "All is well?"

Natasha turned to see Oleg climbing in the window. "All is well," she said.

Just then, they heard a car drive up. Natasha glanced out the window.

"It's Greg and Kelly." Suddenly, she remembered the tissue flowers she was supposed to have been making all evening. "Oh man, I only made one flower—and that one is booger-encrusted!" She picked up a tissue, folded it, and reached for another paper.

Oleg took it from her. "Natasha, no matter

how fast you work, you'll never make enough in time. It's too much for one person to do."

Natasha slumped. "You're right. Guess I'll have to go tell them. Wish me luck."

She found Greg and Kelly arguing on the sofa. She waited until they were through and then cleared her throat. "So, uh, how was the movie?"

"Boring," Greg said with a yawn.

Kelly gave him a nasty look then turned to Natasha. "Where are the flowers?"

"The flowers?" Natasha stammered. "Yes, the flowers. Um . . . "

Kelly narrowed her eyes. "You didn't make them? What have you been doing all night?"

Something bumped behind Natasha. Startled, she turned to see a cardboard box sliding down the stairs. She was even more startled to find it filled with tissue paper flowers!

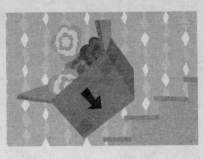

When Kelly saw the flowers, her jaw dropped.

Natasha glanced up the stairs and saw Oleg duck out of sight. "Well, there you are! Um, good night!"

She ran up the stairs, grabbed a grinning Oleg by the collar, and hurried him back to her room. Inside, she found twenty Olegs sitting on her floor making paper flowers.

"Oleg, what have you done?"

"Just a little extra cloning. When they are

done, I will once again reprogram the Zy-Clone to zap them away. Then I will destroy the device so no one can use it again."

"Oh, Oleg, how can I ever repay you?"

"You could buy me some more batteries sometime. I seem to be running low."

"You bet, and thanks, Oleg," Natasha said gratefully. "Now if you don't mind, I have one more favor to ask."

"Yes?"

"Help me get them out of here! After all," she said with a grin, "I think we've done enough cloning around for one night, don't you?"